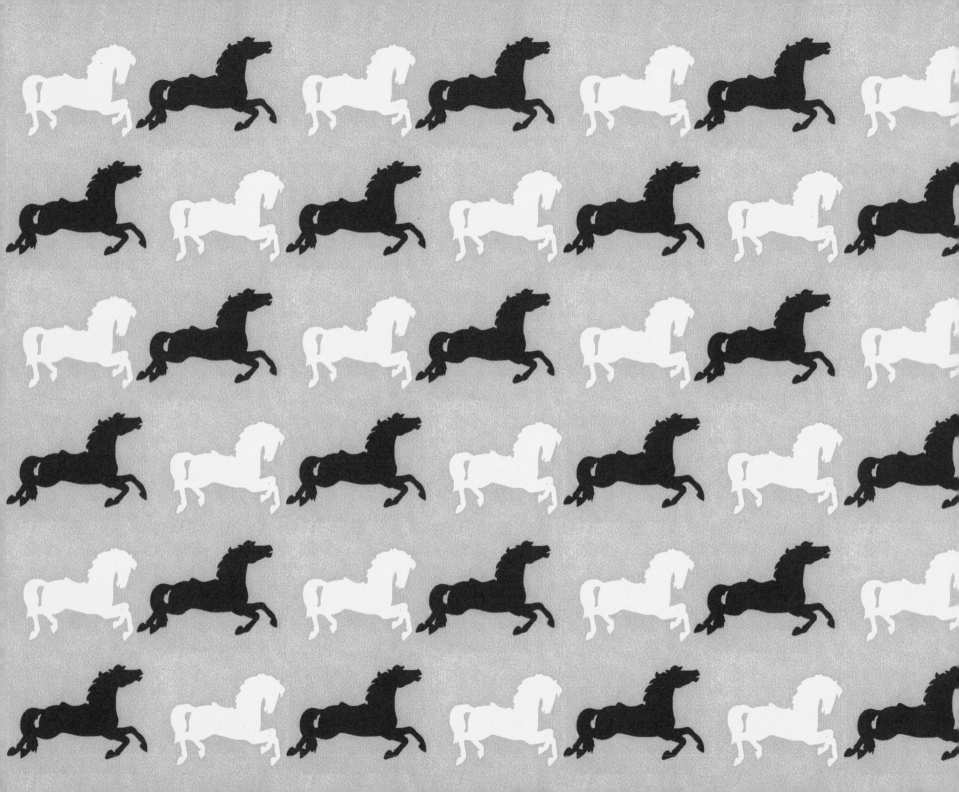

HOW FRANCIS GOT
HIS WINK

Elaine L. Danchey

Janee Hughes

Francis

DEDICATION

To Frank and Mary Catherine Schomus for the inspiration.
To the hundreds of individuals who have donated their
time, money, and talent to make Salem's Riverfront Carousel
a reality. And to Alex for making me believe that love
really can transcend time and place.

A generous donation from Edward H. and Ann Allen helped finance the publication of this book.

Published by
Little America Publishing Company
(an imprint of Beautiful America Publishing Company)
P.O. Box 244, 2600 Progress Way
Woodburn, OR 97071

Design: Anne O'Rourke

Library of Congress Catalog Number 00-042916
ISBN 0-89802-737-3

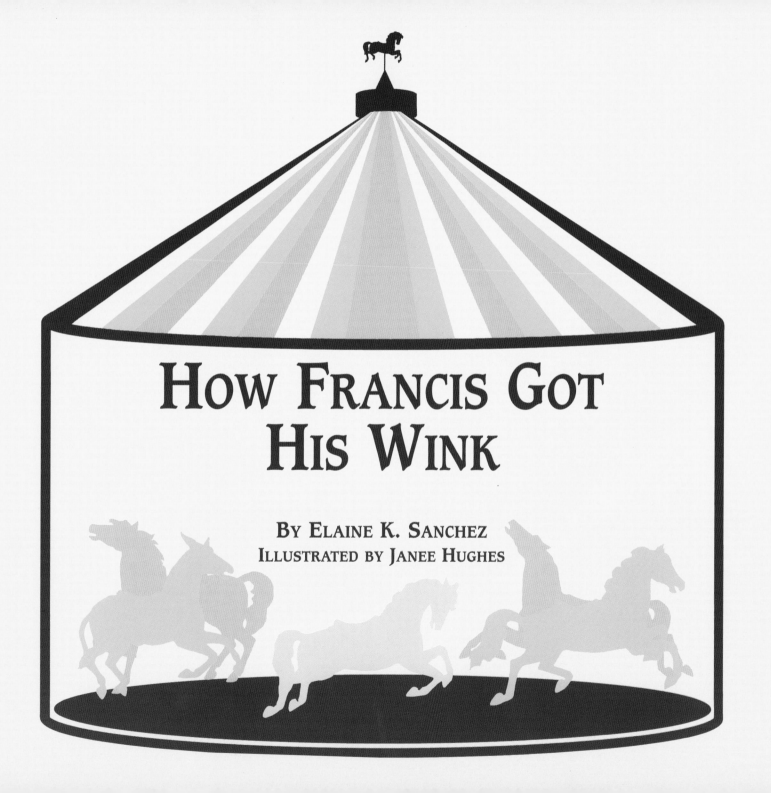

How Francis Got His Wink

By Elaine K. Sanchez
Illustrated by Janee Hughes

Francis turned twelve in the spring of 1921. He hadn't paid much attention to girls, since most of them didn't like worms or toads or his best friend, Harold.

One afternoon, after months of gray skies with low, soggy clouds that oozed rain over the wooded hills and gentle valleys of Salem, Oregon, the sun came out. Vibrant colors exploded from trees and bushes – scarlet camellias, sunshine yellow daffodils, and sweet-smelling grape hyacinths announced the arrival of spring

Harold and Francis raced out of class at the end of the day and headed toward their favorite spot on the Willamette River. Once out of the schoolyard, Harold tugged at Francis's sleeve. "Stop. I want to measure from here."

"Okay," Francis said.

Harold stood up straight and tall, and stuck his chin out past his chest. He rolled his shoulders, he shook his arms, wiggled his fingers, and then took in long gulps of air. Harold's Adam's apple bobbed up and down as he forced the air into his mouth, down his throat, and into his stomach.

Harold swallowed until he looked full as a balloon. The second it appeared he was about to burst, Harold nodded, they both started running, and Harold started burping.

As they approached the end of the block, Harold's face turned red. Francis could see him straining to force the air out of his belly. They passed Mrs. Bentley's mailbox, the previous record, and the rumble still coming out of Harold sounded like low rolling thunder over the Cascades.

Harold fell to the ground sucking for air when they reached the huge oak tree at the corner. Francis danced around his friend, laughing and shouting, "You did it! You did it!"

"Did what?"

Francis turned and saw a girl peeking around the trunk of the tree. She had long, blonde hair that was shiny in the sun. Her eyes were the color of the sky on a bright summer day, and her skin was scrubbed pinky clean.

She was the prettiest girl Francis had ever seen.

"Harold just set a record. That burp was a block long."

"That's disgusting!" she replied, looking at Harold as if he had some sort of disease.

Harold stood up and walked toward the girl slowly, menacingly, until he was so close to her that she pressed her back into the tree trunk. He swallowed several breaths quickly then burped, "Thank you."

The girl shoved Harold on the chest and said, "Get away!"

Harold stepped back laughing, and the girl tossed her hair over her shoulder, tilted her face upward and started walking away quickly.

Francis surprised himself by yelling, "Wait, don't go!"

He was even more surprised when she turned around. "Why should I stay?"

"Because we're going to the river. You can go with us."

"What's at the river?" she asked.

"You're new in town, aren't you?" Francis asked.

She nodded.

"My name's Francis, and this is Harold."

"Francis? Isn't that a girl's name?"

"Nah, he's too ugly to be a girl," Harold kidded.

"What's your name?" Francis asked.

"Mary Catherine."

"I'll call you 'Kate.'"

"Nobody else does," she said.

"They should. It fits you," Francis replied.

"Show her your new face, Francis," Harold said.

"Not now," Francis replied.

"What face is that?" Kate asked.

Francis called it, "The nose-licking-white-eyed ear-wiggler." He wasn't able to burp like Harold, but nobody else could make a face like this one. It was great.

Francis grinned. "Come with us to the river. I'll show you there."

When they reached the cottonwood tree next to a shallow elbow of the Willamette River, they showed Kate the limb that was growing out of the trunk and hanging low over the water. It was as big around as grown man's body.

Francis, Harold, and Kate took off their shoes and socks and piled them next to the base of the tree. Francis took Kate's hand when she stepped onto the limb and was reluctant to let go of it when they all sat down.

Francis dipped his feet into the icy water. He felt tingly sensations in his toes. The cold climbed past his ankles, over his knees and shivered his legs all the way up to his spine.

"Put your feet in," Francis said to Kate through chattering teeth.

She dipped her toes in daintily, but withdrew them quickly, "Yikes! It's freezing!"

"Girls are so dumb," Harold said, "It's melted snow from the mountains. Of course it's cold."

Francis said, "Shut up, Harold."

Then he turned to Kate and asked, "Do you want to see my face now?"

"I guess," she said, still looking a little mad.

"Here goes." Francis stood up on the branch, held out his hand to Kate and pulled her up. He stood facing her, put his hands on his skinny hips, stretched his neck forward, and stuck his tongue out so far that the little strip of skin underneath it was strained so tight it felt like a rubber band ready to snap. Then pushing his bottom jaw forward, he rolled his tongue upward and licked the tip of his nose. At the same time Francis rolled his eyes back in his head until all that showed were the whites, and then he wiggled his ears.

"Oh yuk! You're as gross as Harold. I'm leaving."

Francis grabbed her hands.

"Let go of me," she hissed. "You're disgusting!"

Francis didn't release his grip. "I don't want you to fall in the water." He backed up slowly on the huge limb, but held on.

Kate narrowed her eyes at him. "I said, let me go!"

"Not until I get you back on the shore."

Harold was laughing. "Better let him help you, Kate. Besides being ugly and disgusting, Francis is as stubborn as a mule."

"Well, he's as stupid as a mule if he thinks he can stop me."

Francis grinned at Kate and said, "I may be stubborn, and I may be ugly, but I'm not stupid."

"You wanna bet?"

"Yeah. I'll bet someday you're gonna be my girl." Then he winked at her.

Kate's face turned red. She opened her mouth to say something, but she just sputtered. She pushed past Francis and stomped off.

Francis was sixteen the summer Harold moved away. It was the saddest day of his life. Francis had helped load Harold's family's things onto the truck, and now the boys were standing in the street, kicking dirt clods down the hill.

Harold's dad closed the heavy doors on the back of the truck, then he hiked himself up behind the wheel and called for Harold to get in. Harold said, "Well, I guess this is it."

Francis swallowed hard, afraid he might cry. "I don't know what to say."

Harold didn't say anything, he just started swallowing huge gulps of air as he climbed into the passenger seat.

The truck strained to gain speed under the weight of its load, and it jerked and lurched every time Harold's dad shifted gears. Francis ran alongside, keeping even until his legs ached and he thought his lungs might burst. When they reached the crest of the hill, Harold leaned out the window, let loose with a full body belch and waved goodbye.

Francis tried to keep up, but the truck gained speed going down hill, and in less than a minute it reached the bottom of the steep slope. Harold was still leaning out the window waving as the truck rounded the corner and disappeared from sight.

Harold was gone.

Francis walked to the old cottonwood tree on the Willamette. He climbed out on the branch and sat, looking into the river, wondering why people had to change jobs and move away.

Francis heard a soft voice behind him. "You look like you've just lost your best friend."

He turned around and saw Kate standing on the bank. "I have. Harold's moving to Seattle."

"I'm sorry."

"Yeah, me too."

Kate walked out on the branch and sat down next to Francis. "It's hard to say goodbye to someone you love," Kate said.

"Harold was a guy. I didn't love him."

"Boys are so stupid. There's all sorts of love – not just the kind between men and women."

"You might be right," Francis conceded, as he watched small brown ripples of river water pass beneath their dangling feet.

"My grandma says if you hold love and good memories of a person in your heart, they're never really gone."

"Do you believe that?" Francis asked.

"Maybe."

"I don't know, I sure feel lonely right now."

"I'll be your friend," Kate offered and she patted his knee.

Francis turned and looked at Kate. "Will you be my girl?" he asked.

"I don't know you well enough to be your girl."

"That's not true. We've known each other for four years. Besides, I know you're nice and I know you're pretty. Isn't that enough?"

"I'll have to think about that," she replied.

"Will you think about being my girl?"

"You don't give up, do you?"

Francis grinned and said, "I'm stubborn as a mule." Then he winked.

Kate and Francis did become best friends. They walked in the woods, they fished in the river. They had picnics in fields of flowers in the summer, and they went to movies on rainy winter evenings.

And one summer night, when they were grown, the moon was full, and the sky was clear, Francis said, "Kate, I love you. I want you to be my girl forever."

"Forever is a long time, Francis."

"It won't be long enough," he said.

Then he grinned and winked.

Kate kissed his cheek and said, "I'll be proud to be your wife, Francis."

The years passed. Francis and Kate built a home for their family. Francis was a wonderful carpenter. He loved wood. He thought he could smell the forest in every piece he sawed.

When their first baby was born Francis selected the finest pieces of lumber, sanded them down smooth, and made a fine crib. Kate used bits of brightly colored fabric and stitched colorful quilts for the tiny bed.

Francis built their home strong, and Kate decorated it with flowers from her garden.

As time went by, the children grew up and moved away, and one day Francis looked in the mirror and realized he was old. He didn't feel old, but he had wrinkles on his face, and his hair was thin and gray.

Sometimes when Kate kidded him about being a stubborn old mule, he would hum the song, "The old gray mare, she ain't what she used to be."

One day Kate became ill and Francis took her to see the doctor. Every day they hoped Kate would feel better, but her sweet, old heart was worn out, and one night, while she slept, it just quit beating.

When Francis walked through Kate's flower beds, he'd always stop to admire the yellow calla lilies and the pansies – Kate's favorites. And whenever he sat down in his chair, he'd pull a quilt onto his lap. Kate's hands had been there. Her fingers had pushed the needle through the fabric and pulled it back through to create intricate patterns.

He was so lonely.

One day as Francis was reading the newspaper while eating breakfast, he learned a carousel was being built for the children of the Willamette Valley. The volunteers planned to build 41 horses, all of them hand carved and painted. Each horse would need an adoptive family to help pay for the carousel.

Francis didn't even finish his eggs. He pushed the newspaper aside, got his keys, and drove straight to the carving studio.

As he walked through the tables where volunteers were working, he breathed in the scent of the wood. Francis watched as the carvers edged their blades into the wood and chiseled away. Some were chipping small hunks, others were peeling long, thin strips that fell in curlicues at their feet.

Francis found Dave, the head carver, and described the horse he wanted built. She would be beautiful and feminine, with a light silvery coat. She'd have a quilt for the saddle blanket, and there would be flowers intertwined on her trappings. She would be called "Kate."

It took months of planning, drawing, carving, sanding, and painting, but finally it was done.

Dave, Francis, and a lot of other volunteers worked on Kate's horse, and she was beautiful; but there was something wrong. Francis left the studio feeling disappointed and empty inside. Before he got to his car he knew what was missing. He walked back to the studio, found Dave and told him he wanted to adopt another horse. When Francis described what he wanted, Dave wasn't sure he liked the idea, but Francis, true to his nature, was stubborn, and the carving began.

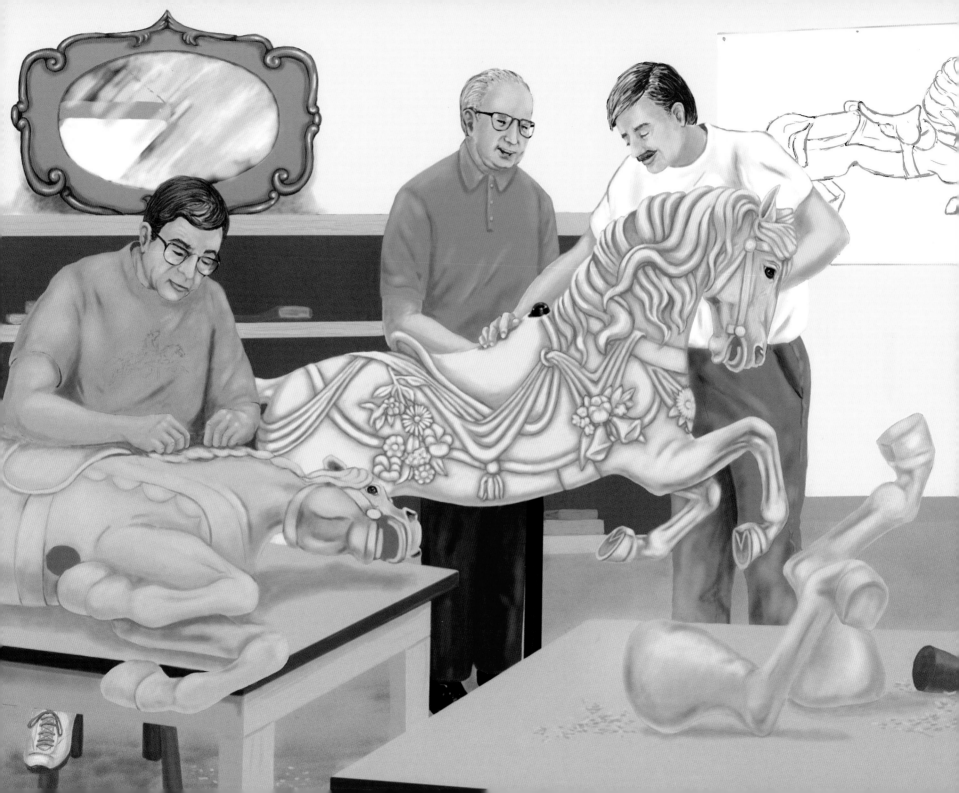

Volunteers worked thousands of hours carving and painting the horses, raising money, and constructing the building, and finally one bright summer day, Salem's Riverfront Carousel opened to the public.

Francis had followed the parade through Salem's downtown to Riverfront Park and found a bench next to the Carousel. Kate was so delicate and light it looked as if she might float away when she started her circular flight. And there, right next to her stood an ugly old brown mule. His eyebrows were carved slanting down toward the long snout, and the top lip curled in a snarl. The mule was named Francis, and his expression was so stubborn and cross that it made Francis chuckle.

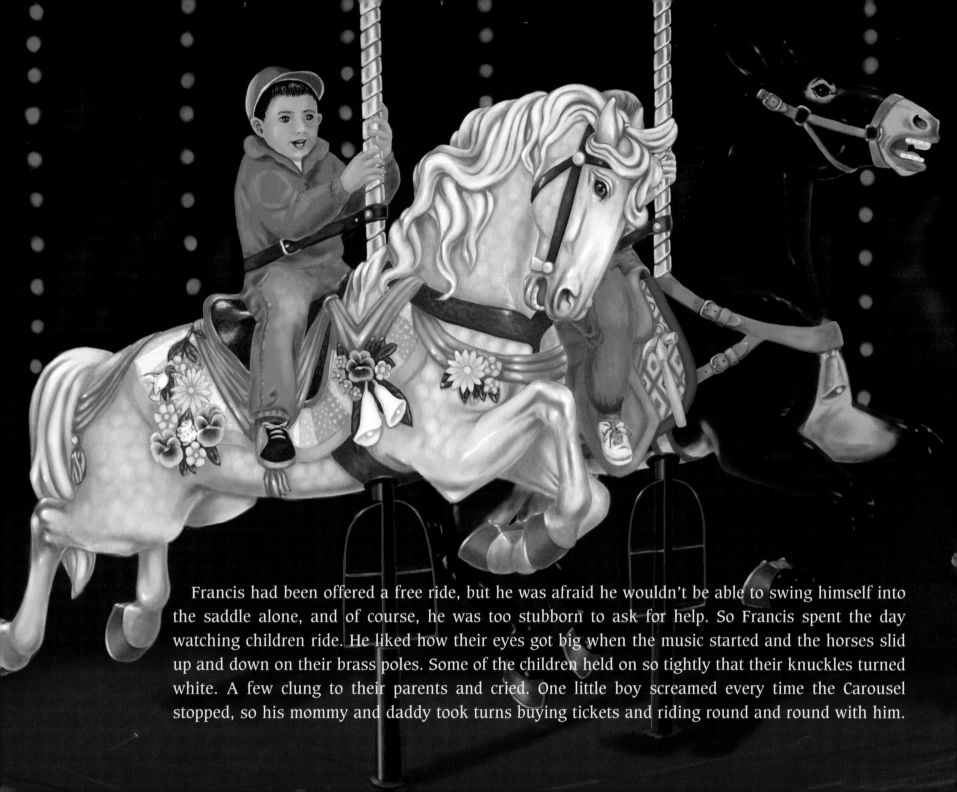

Francis had been offered a free ride, but he was afraid he wouldn't be able to swing himself into the saddle alone, and of course, he was too stubborn to ask for help. So Francis spent the day watching children ride. He liked how their eyes got big when the music started and the horses slid up and down on their brass poles. Some of the children held on so tightly that their knuckles turned white. A few clung to their parents and cried. One little boy screamed every time the Carousel stopped, so his mommy and daddy took turns buying tickets and riding round and round with him.

The Carousel project had brought hundreds of volunteers together, now it was bringing families together. Francis wished Kate could have seen it.

When the sun set and the celebration ended, people gathered up their children and headed home. The music stopped, the Carousel stood still, the volunteers laughed, hugged and congratulated each other, and one by one, they all left the park.

Everyone except Francis. He sat alone on the bench, watched the twilight turn to dark and listened as the breeze rippled through the leaves of the cottonwood trees next to the river.

Finally, he decided to go also. But he wanted to say good night to Kate first. His old legs wobbled a little when he stood up, and he was careful not to stumble when he climbed up on the Carousel and walked to Kate's horse. He leaned against her, stroking her face and mane gently.

He heard a soft voice. "Climb on."

Startled, Francis turned around. "Who's there?"

"Don't be stubborn, Francis. Just get on the mule."

"Is that you, Kate?"

"Yes, Francis. It's me. Climb on and we'll go for a ride."

Francis's heart was pounding and he wondered if he'd gone crazy as he heaved himself into the saddle.

"Over here," she said.

There she was, on top of her horse. She looked just as she had the day he met her – young, healthy, and full of life. Her blue eyes twinkled just as he remembered.

Kate was laughing. "You wanna play?"

"You bet!" Francis yelled.

Kate nudged her horse in the ribs with her heels and off they flew into the night sky. They climbed high over the trees growing along the bank of the Willamette, then they swooped down like birds and skimmed over the shallow elbow of the river where their favorite cottonwood still stood. Kate slowed her horse, and Francis came to a stop next to her.

Francis was out of breath when he asked, "Is this real?"

"It's magic, Francis, but we only have until dawn."

"What happens then?"

"I'll tell you later."

"Okay, let's go, then!" Francis shouted.

They took off, following the Willamette, racing past trees, houses, buildings, and leaping high over bridges and boats.

"I'll race you to the waterfalls," Kate shouted.

"Go for it!"

They galloped across the night sky, and landed on a soft bed of pine needles at Silver Creek Falls. They walked the path side by side, holding hands, stopping at each waterfall to listen and look. They walked in the creek to South Falls where the water rushed over the ledge with a thunderous roar dropping a hundred feet to the pool below. They peered over the edge.

"Do you want to slide down?" Kate asked.

"Won't it kill us?"

"No, silly. It's magic, remember? Come on, slide with me."

They urged their horses forward, stepped off the ledge and swoosh – they were swept along in the falling water like they were on a giant slippery slide. They landed softly in the pool below, and laughed as the water poured over their heads.

They climbed down from their horses, walked up the bank and shook themselves like dogs, splattering water all around. They laughed and hugged, then walked some more. Kate's horse and Francis's mule shuffled behind them stopping occasionally to munch on tender fern leaves.

"Francis, do you remember a long time ago when I told you that if you hold a person in your heart they're never really gone?"

"The day Harold moved away," Francis replied.

"That's right. I've seen him, you know."

"You've seen Harold? I thought he died in the war."

"He did, but he's fine now – still ornery though. You know all those years you thought cucumbers made you burp?"

"It wasn't the cucumbers?"

Kate shook her head, smiling. "It was Harold."

"No kidding. Just like him," Francis chuckled. "I'd love to see him again."

"You will someday." They walked along the path quietly for a few moments.

"You know something else, Francis? At night when you pull the quilt up close around your neck and it feels all soft and warm?"

"Yeah," Francis replied.

"That's me. I'm right there with you every night when you go to sleep." She touched the tips of her fingers to his cheek. "I'm always with you, Francis. I'm in your heart, remember?"

"Don't go away again, Kate. Please don't," he pleaded.

They stopped in a patch of maidenhair ferns. She squeezed his hand and said, "It's time for us to leave."

"I don't want to."

"I know Francis, but our horses have to be back in their places by sunrise."

"What if they're not?"

"They'll be frozen in time."

"What do you mean?"

"Wherever they are, and whatever they're doing the moment the sun comes up, is where they'll stay for eternity."

"Good! Let's stay here. Kate, I miss you. I don't want this night to end. I want to go with you."

"You can't, Francis. God isn't ready for you yet."

"Why not?"

"There are things I can't explain. You just have to trust me and follow the rules."

"I don't like the rules."

Kate stamped her foot. "Francis, you are being so stubborn! It wouldn't be fair to the wood carvers and the painters or the children if our horses disappeared from the Carousel. We have to leave now. Don't argue with me!" Kate climbed back on her silvery steed, and Francis followed on his mule.

It was starting to get light in the east as they raced back to Salem. Kate yelled, "Francis, we stayed too long! Please don't dilly-dally. Hurry, go faster!"

The clouds were taking on color from the rising sun, and they were billowing up like huge mountains of pink cotton candy. Francis didn't want to go back to Salem, but he didn't want Kate to be mad at him, so he urged his mule to fly faster.

The sky was bright when they arrived at the Carousel. The clouds had turned from pink to a fiery orange as the sun drew closer to the horizon.

Breathing heavily, Kate led her horse into its place on the Carousel. Francis followed, guiding his mule next to her horse. Kate turned to him and said, "Thank you, Francis, for remembering me this way."

"You're welcome," he said. Kate was looking a little blurry. Francis figured it was because of the tears in his eyes.

"Don't be sad. Come on, give me one more grin and wink."

"You'll always be my girl, Kate."

A single tear slid down his cheek as Francis winked at her, but he managed a grin at the exact moment the sun lifted itself above the horizon and into the morning sky.

Francis heard voices. He opened his eyes. It was morning. He was sitting on the bench next to the Carousel. What was he doing on the bench?

Oh no! It was just a dream. But it seemed so real. He had talked with her, held her hand, kissed her. He didn't want it to be a dream.

Francis looked up to see a tall maintenance man in a brown uniform loading trash bags into the back of a pickup. Another worker was on the Carousel standing next to Kate's horse and Francis's mule. He had a sponge in his hand, and was wiping away sticky fingerprints and smudges of dirt. He shouted, "Hey, would you look at this?"

"What is it?" the tall man asked.

"Look at this mule would you? Something's wrong with his eye. He's squinting."

The maintenance man came over to take a look. "That's funny. He didn't look like that yesterday. I remember thinking he was an ugly, stubborn old mule. He looked grouchy. But look at the stupid grin on his face now."

Francis ran to the Carousel. "Let me see!" he exclaimed, pushing his way past both workers.

Francis examined the mule carefully, then started to laugh. "Boys, this mule may be stubborn, and he may be ugly, but he's not stupid!"

"Why do you say that?" asked the worker with the sponge.

"Look at him. He's winking at the prettiest filly on the Carousel."

SALEM'S RIVERFRONT CAROUSEL

In 1996, Hazel Patton visited Missoula, Montana where she saw the first old-world style carousel built in the U.S. since the Great Depression. While impressed with the ornately carved and hand-painted horses, she discovered the real beauty was how the carousel had united that community by combining local history with the creative talents of Missoula's citizens. It has been Hazel's vision and dedication that has brought Salem's Riverfront Carousel to the banks of the Willamette.

Since that time, Salem's Riverfront Carousel project has brought together a diversified group of volunteers, including Dave and Sandy Walker. Together they have directed the creative efforts of hundreds of woodcarvers and painters. Sandy, a talented artist, met with the 41 adopters and designed the horses and symbols that represent each family and business. In addition, she has led the group of artists who have painted the horses and various other carvings on the Carousel. Dave, a master carver, trained most of the woodcarvers and has overseen thousands of hours of loving, but painstaking work.

The vision of Salem's Riverfront Carousel is to touch the hearts, spark the imaginations, and ignite the creative spirits of a broad spectrum of volunteers by creating a work of art that will stand as an historical landmark and an enduring symbol of community pride and cooperation.

All of the volunteers, including artists, carvers, writers, musicians, general contractors, and business specialists, hope you will come visit Salem's Riverfront Carousel. There's something magical about climbing up high on a wooden horse, listening for the organ music to begin, and anticipating the tummy tickles that are inevitable when the Carousel starts to move and the horses take off on their circular flights.

ABOUT THE AUTHOR

After retiring from a career in television advertising, Elaine Sanchez moved with her husband, Alex, from Albuquerque, New Mexico to Salem, Oregon in the summer of 1998. She decided to pursue her dream of writing at that time. She has published a short story entitled, "The Last Carving," and is currently working on a novel.

Believing that life is short and the world is large, Elaine and Alex enjoy traveling and spending time with their kids and grandkids. Elaine has been an active volunteer with the Carousel project, serving on the board of directors and several committees, including writing, marketing, and fund raising.

ABOUT THE ILLUSTRATOR

Since retiring from 31 years of teaching art to middle school students, Janee Hughes has been pursuing a freelance career. She has won awards for her equine art, and has illustrated magazines, newspapers and catalogs.

Janee has been a dedicated volunteer on the Carousel project. She has donated her time and talents by painting the Carousel horses and shields. She created a limited edition poster entitled "Hero's Wish," which is being sold as a fund raiser for Salem's Riverfront Carousel.

Although Janee usually paints with watercolors or acrylics, she used a computer program to paint the illustrations in this book.

Janee and her husband, Bill, live on acreage east of Salem where they enjoy caring for their two horses.

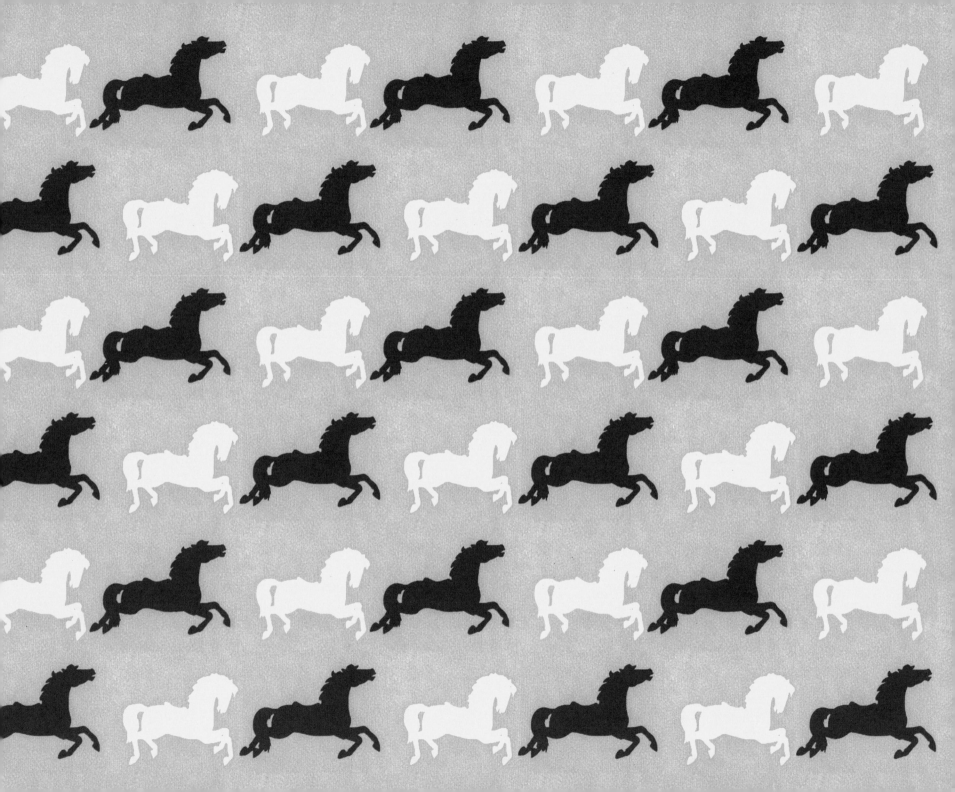

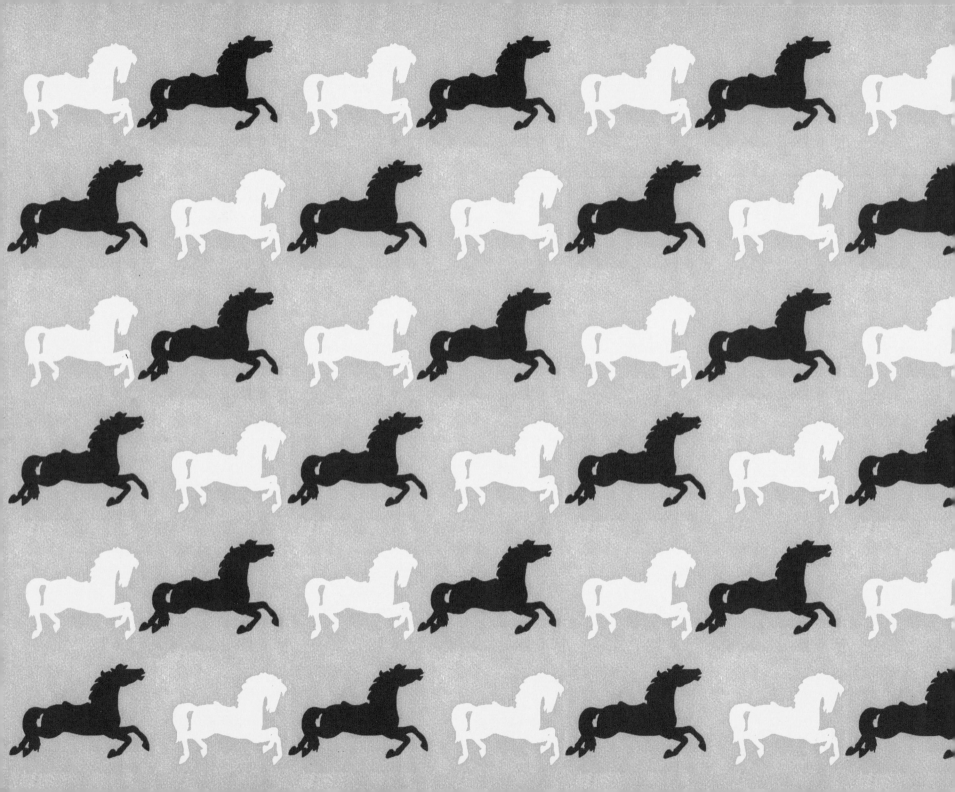